The English Roses are five of the B.F.E.

The English Roses

Being Binah

CALLAWAY ARTS & ENTERTAINMENT
19 FULTON STREET, FIFTH FLOOR, NEW YORK, NEW YORK 10038

PUFFIN BOOKS
Published by the Penguin Group
Penguin Young Readers Group, 345 Hudson Street, New York, New York 10014, U.S.A.
Penguin Group (Canada), 90 Eglinton Avenue East, Suite 700, Toronto, Ontario,
Canada M4P2Y3 (a division of Pearson Penguin Canada Inc.)

Penguin Books Ltd., Registered Offices: 80 Strand, London WC2R 0RL, England

First published in the United States of America by Callaway Arts & Entertainment and Puffin Books, 2008

1 3 5 7 9 10 8 6 4 2

First Edition

Produced by Callaway Arts & Entertainment
Nicholas Callaway, President and Publisher
Cathy Ferrara, Managing Editor and Production Director
Toshiya Masuda, Art Director • Nelson Gómez, Director of Digital Technology
Joya Rajadhyaksha, Editor • Amy Cloud, Editor
Ivan Wong, Jr. and José Rodríguez, Production
Kathryn Bradwell, Executive Assistant to the Publisher
Jennifer Caffrey, Publishing Assistant

Special thanks to Doug Whiteman and Mariann Donato.

Library of Congress Cataloging-in-Publication Data is available.

Puffin Books ISBN 978-0-14-241095-0

Printed in the United States of America

www.madonna.com www.callaway.com www.penguin.com/youngreaders

All of Madonna's proceeds from this book will be donated to
Raising Malawi (www.raisingmalawi.org), an orphan-care initiative.

The English Roses

by MADONNA

with Erica Ottenberg

Being Binah

illustrated by jeffrey fulvimari

PUFFIN
CALLAWAY
New York
2008

Book 6

Contents

Don't Even! 7

Slam! 15

Hello, Ben 21

Enter Evelyn Eaves 35

Lizzie Love 45

The Importance of Sketching Ernest 55

A Halo of Frizz 65

A Girl Thing 77

The New Binah 83

In Her Shoes 93

Not So Boring 103

Roses to the Rescue! 111

One More Surprise 115

CHAPTER I

Don't Even!

You have most certainly heard of the English Roses by now. If not, the only logical explanation is that you were abducted by aliens and have been living on a far-away planet, only returning to find that you don't know the hottest fingernail polish colors, the latest fashion trends, or, most importantly, the English Roses. Well, it's understandable. You've been away! So welcome back. And let's remedy this situation right away, shall we?

The English Roses are five of the BFE (that's "best friends ever"—See, you're learning already!): Charlotte Ginsberg, Amy Brook, Grace Harrison, Nicole Rissman, and Binah Rossi. Five girls as

different as different can be. But they're there for each other through thick and thin, up and down, high and low. And there is never a shortage of thick, thin, up, down, high, or low. After all, they are in the sixth grade, which can be quite an adventure. And the English Roses always seem to be right in the thick of the action.

This particular morning, however, had been relatively uneventful.

By the time the lunch bell rang, the students burst out through the school's front doors like water exploding through a dam. You see, sunny days at Hampstead School meant not only football scrimmages, but outdoor lunch hour as well. The girls trouped across campus, trying not to get trampled by their peers.

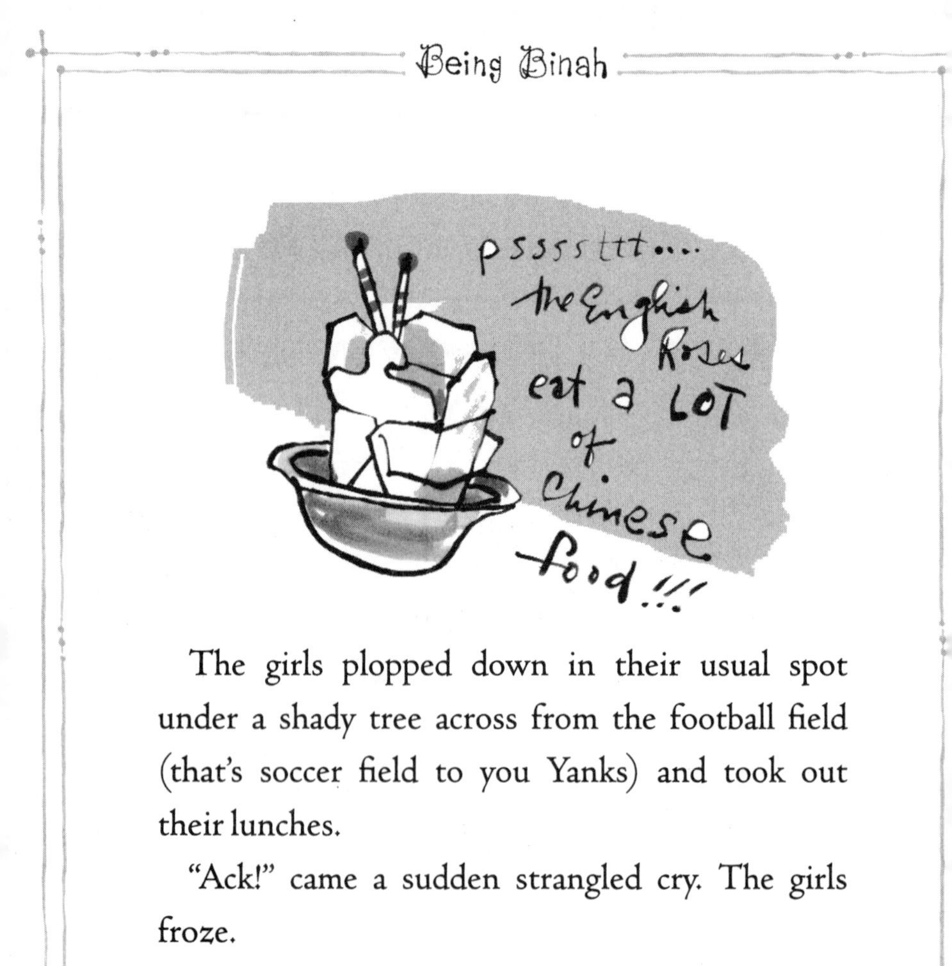

The girls plopped down in their usual spot under a shady tree across from the football field (that's soccer field to you Yanks) and took out their lunches.

"Ack!" came a sudden strangled cry. The girls froze.

"Did that sound come from a person?" Grace asked.

Amy looked up, her face contorted into a sour expression. "These Chinese leftovers from last night are most definitely lacking something," she said disgustedly.

"Gross!" Charlotte squealed. "Don't even!"

"Don't even!" was Charlotte's latest favorite phrase. She adopted a new one every few months. It never really meant anything specific, but she found a way to apply it to almost any situation. "Don't even!" had recently replaced "Do you love it?" as the phrase-du-jour.

The girls giggled.

"Ha, ha, very funny," Amy said. "I'm starving. And I can't possibly force this down." She gestured halfheartedly to the noodles in front of her.

Suddenly, Nicole lit up. "Hey, Charlie," she said. "Don't you usually keep some soy sauce in your locker for emergencies?"

Charlotte grinned. "As a matter of fact, I do!" she said. "Nicole, what would we do without you?"

Amy looked disappointed. "Great idea," she said, somewhat sheepishly. "But by the time I go all the

way back inside to get it, I'll miss Ryan Hudson's turn in the game."

The girls exchanged humorous looks. Ryan Hudson was Amy's Big Crush.

Binah smiled. "Don't worry," she said. "I'll run back and get it for you."

Amy turned to her friend. "Really? Are you sure?"

Binah nodded. "Of course! I don't mind at all."

"Of course she doesn't mind," said Grace. "Binah's . . ."

". . . The nice one!" the rest of the girls chorused together.

"We'll save you a spot in the shade," Amy said gratefully. With a wave, Binah headed back inside.

CHAPTER 2

Slam!

Is there anything quite like the quiet of an empty school hallway? Binah's footsteps echoed—*click, click, click*—as she made her way back to Mrs. Moss's classroom. She felt as if she was the only person left in a deserted world. She fleetingly wondered if she might never see another living person again. She shivered at the thought, then shook it off. How silly she was; it was just an empty hallway. Binah walked on.

"Hello?" she asked softly as she eased open the door to Mrs. Moss's classroom. There sat her teacher, bent over her big wooden desk, papers piled almost all the way up to the wire-rimmed glasses perched on the tip of her rather long, thin nose. She barely looked up as she shuffled files and scribbled notes with her trademark red pen.

"Hi, Mrs. Moss," Binah said. Or, rather, whispered. Binah's shyness tended to multiply whenever she was around teachers. That is, teachers except for Miss Fluffernutter, her favorite from last year. Miss Fluffernutter was so . . . Fluffernuttery! Sometimes you forgot she even was a teacher.

Mrs. Moss finally noticed that there was someone else in the room. She emitted a preoccupied "Harrumph" that Binah took to mean "Can't you

see I'm busy? Pease don't bother me." So Binah said no more. She quickly tiptoed back to the coatroom, where she and her classmates stored their jackets and book bags and gym shoes during the school day.

She soon found Charlotte's bag and began rifling through for the all-important soy sauce. She'd just found it when all of a sudden—

SLAM!!!!

Binah gasped and whirled around. The room was now pitch-dark, the slammed door echoing in the blackness. What on earth had happened? Where was Mrs. Moss? She willed herself to steady her frightened breathing as she edged along the row of cubbies, turning the corner to step into the now dark and empty classroom. Mrs. Moss was gone.

She was alone.

moss
says
moss
BE ALERT OR ELSE!
don't
Forget
!!!
19

CHAPTER 3

Hello, Ben

Have you ever had the feeling that you want to cry—that you should be crying—only the tears won't come? Well, that is exactly how Binah felt as she stood alone in a dark and empty classroom. She was frozen in fear, and she felt that her tears must be frozen in her eyes. What was she supposed to do? Mrs. Moss had . . . forgotten her! She almost couldn't believe it. Fear began to melt into indignation (which was a vocab quiz word Mrs. Moss's red pen had recently informed her meant "righteous anger or resentment." Nicole, who had never missed a vocab quiz question in her life, further elaborated that it is what one feels when one has been wronged by someone else, like when Mrs. Moss yells at Charlotte for talking in class when it was her troublemaking seatmate, William Worthington, who had started talking to her in the first place!). Her teacher had literally forgotten she existed in the few minutes it took Binah to walk past her to the coatroom!

As her cheeks burned in frustration, something happened that was even more terrifying than being left in the classroom with all the lights turned off. For just then, in front of Binah's eyes, the doorknob began to turn. Binah took a step back. The handle moved. She jumped behind a desk. It twisted some more. She knelt on the ground. The latch made a sickening click. And then, as a trembling Binah cowered behind a chair, the door flew open. So Binah flew into action.

Smash! went Charlotte's soy sauce as Binah sent it shattering to the floor, half in fear, half in self-defense. She let out a gaspy shriek and darted to the back of the room. But the hem of her skirt

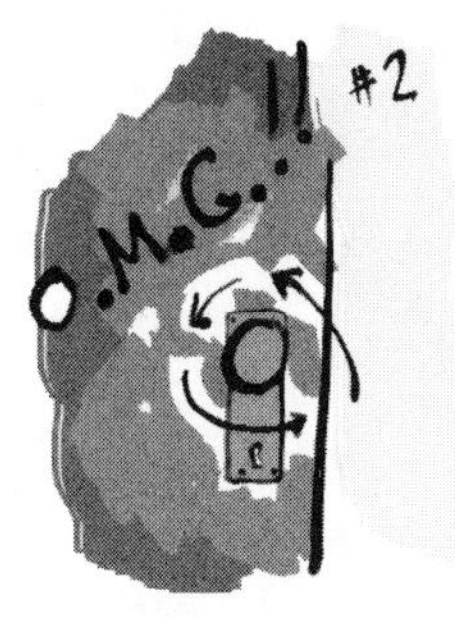

caught on the edge of the desk she'd hid behind, and instead of fleeing into the coatroom, she was sent sprawling to the floor, where she lay, her head buried in her hands, waiting for whatever horrible fate was sure to befall her.

"Um, hi." A voice! "Hey . . . are you OK?" A voice that did not seem intent on doing her bodily harm. Binah lifted her head. The lights flicked on. "I'm sorry. I didn't mean to startle you. I was just . . ."

Binah sat up and surveyed the damage. Her shirt was ripped and half untucked, and there were

unseemly soy sauce stains on her skirt. Not to mention giant holes in her sleeves where she'd skidded across the gritty floor. Her hands fluttered to her legs as she attempted to smooth her skirt. "No! No, it's fine. I'm sorry, it's my fault. I just . . . wasn't expecting anyone."

The boy with the nice voice reached out a very helpful hand. Binah hesitated for a moment, then let him pull her to her feet.

"Hey there, Binah," said Ben.

"Hi . . . Ben," Binah replied.

He looked down at the soy sauce–stained hand he was still holding. "You're sure you're all right?"

Binah blushed. She'd never actually talked to this boy, though lately she'd thought about doing so quite often. He'd always been there, sitting quietly in the back of the classroom, seemingly content to let others do the volunteering. Much like Binah herself. In fact, she hadn't really noticed him at all until a few months ago. They'd been walking out of the room one day after class had ended. Binah had been hurrying to catch up with her friends when Ben had brushed by her on his way out the door. He'd passed her desk and then turned, smiled at her, and stood to the side to let her pass in front of him. To some that would have been the smallest, most inconsequential action. But to Binah it had been a gesture of grand proportions. After that, she took notice of him quite a bit. She noticed his shaggy brown hair that always seemed to find its way into his eyes. She noticed the way he squinched up his nose to inch his tortoiseshell glasses back into place when they slid down too far, as they often did. She noticed the way he always rolled the sleeves of his button-down shirts up to his elbows and how he'd rub his fingers over a small constellation of freckles on his forearm when he was thinking hard about something. She noticed herself noticing a lot of things about him that no one else seemed to—apparently his shyly sweet demeanor and un-in-your-face cuteness had yet to catch anyone else's interest.

Right now, however, she noticed just what an absolute mess she was! She tried to straighten her skirt without being too obvious about it. "I'm fine, really. Please. I'll just . . ." Her stomach was doing somersaults. She was suddenly quite thankful she hadn't yet eaten lunch, as it seemed that anything she'd ingested might be making a sudden reappearance in the near future.

"Why don't I help you clean this up?" Ben suggested, gesturing to the soy sauce–stained floor. He grabbed some paper towels from the sink and

handed a few to Binah. When his hand brushed against hers, Binah felt a slight tremor inside her.

"You don't have to go," Ben said once they had mopped up the mess. He ran a hand through his hair and adjusted his glasses. "I was just going to feed Ernest. Do you want to help?"

Ernest was the sixth–grade class gerbil. Mrs. Moss had reluctantly agreed to keep him after Alvin Edmonds brought him to school one day, claiming his housekeeper had threatened to flush him down the toilet if she caught him burrowing through her fresh laundry one more time. At first Mrs. Moss had strongly objected, but the class had pleaded with all its might. There were even tears from Carole James, who had an impressive ability to cry on cue. ((WHaaaaH!!!))

"Mrs. Moss appointed me Official Class Gerbil Feeder."

"Oh," said Binah. *Oh? That's the best you can do?* She silently chastised herself for her suddenly very limited vocabulary.

"It's a tough job, but someone's got to do it!" Ben said. His hair fell into his eyes, and he brushed it off his forehead. Every time he did so his glasses slid down his nose, and he'd do that face-scrunching thing to maneuver them back into place. Binah found herself smiling.

Gerbil feeding time is the right time!

"You're probably really impressed," Ben continued. "I mean, not everyone can say they're the Official Class Gerbil Feeder." Binah giggled, and immediately blushed. She opened her mouth, but it was as if her brain had suddenly emptied itself of words. Has that ever happened to you? It's very frustrating and tends to occur precisely at the moment you wish you had the most to say!

"Uh-huh," she stammered.

Ben held up a jar filled with unappetizing-looking brown pellets. "Do you . . . want to help? I could use an Official Class Gerbil Feeder's Assistant."

Binah gulped. Unable to think of a single friendly reply, she backed away and stammered, "Oh . . . no, that's OK. Outside . . . I should be getting . . . for lunch . . . my friends . . ." In reality, there was nothing more Binah would rather have done at that moment than feed pellets to a rodent. But when Ben's eyes met hers, she quickly averted them and made for the door.

"Sorry again," she murmured as she made a beeline for the exit.

"No problem. Nice talking to you, Binah!" Ben called after her. She nodded and ducked through the doorway. *Really nice*, she thought.

CHAPTER 4

Enter Evelyn Eaves

"Does, too!"

"Does not!"

"Does, too!" Amy turned. "Doesn't Mary-Kate have way better fashion sense than Ashley?" she implored Binah, who'd just found her friends by the tree, where they'd set up for lunch.

"Amy, you are the only person on earth who thinks that a raggedy old blanket can be high fashion," Charlotte interjected.

Amy gestured to her own skirt. "This used to be the upholstery on our couch!" she announced proudly. "So there!"

"Wow—impressive, Amy!" Grace leaned in for a closer look. "You'd never know your skirt used to be furniture!" The girls laughed. Binah cleared her throat.

"Hi guys—" she started.

"Binah, what happened to you?" Charlotte interrupted, noticing Binah's rumpled, soy sauce–stained appearance for the first time.

"I—had a bit of an accident. The soy sauce—"

"Oh, don't worry about that," said Amy. "Turns

out Mum threw in some extra soy sauce packets. Crisis averted!"

The bell rang. Binah's stomach growled, and she looked longingly at her uneaten lunch. *Oh well,* she thought. *There's always dinner.*

For the rest of the afternoon, Binah had a hard time concentrating on schoolwork. It seemed as if everything that caught her attention reminded her of her lunchtime "liaison" (which, Nicole would be quick to point out, means "encounter," which basically means "brief meeting with someone who

tends to fill your stomach with butterflies and makes you turn red and unable to come up with anything more interesting to say than "Oh'").

"Did you see what Evelyn Eaves was wearing today?" asked Amy as the girls headed back up the hill to school. "It was to die for! I love that color. It's not purple; it's more like indigo."

"Her skirt was so short!" Nicole chimed in. "I can't believe Mrs. Moss didn't make her change into her gym clothes."

"And what would have been wrong with that?" Grace asked, striking a pose in her Puma jacket and striped mesh shorts.

Nicole smiled. "Nothing at all," she replied.

"It doesn't matter what she wears. Evelyn Eaves could come to school in a paper bag, and the boys would still line up for her," Charlotte pouted. "It's not fair. I don't really see what all the fuss is about, personally."

"I'll admit, she's not the best student. But she's always raising her hand. She definitely knows how to make a name for herself," Nicole said, and shrugged.

"She isn't a pushover, either." Grace winced. "Did you see her in tennis today? Even I couldn't keep up. She's not afraid to show her strength. I think that's kinda cool. And apparently, so do all the guys at Hampstead."

"I know!" Charlotte threw up her hands. "And she's not even nice to them! She has all those adoring fans, and she just ignores them! Maybe that's the secret. If you like someone, be mean."

A rare moment of silence followed as the girls walked on. They glanced at Binah, who'd been awfully quiet up to this point.

"Binah? Care to weigh in?"

Charlotte tapped her lightly on the shoulder, and Binah was jolted out of her reverie. It wasn't that she was ignoring her friends. It was just that she was a little . . . preoccupied. By a certain someone with a mop of brown hair and tortoiseshell glasses and a fondness for hungry gerbils.

"Weigh in?"

"Yeah. What are your thoughts on Evelyn Eaves?"

Binah paused for a moment. "I don't know. . . . I think she's lovely."

At that, the English Roses burst into appreciative laughter.

"That's our Binah!" Amy exclaimed. The girls exchanged smiling glances as they all—all but Binah, that is—chimed in: "You're the nice one!"

CHAPTER 5

Lizzie Love

The next morning, Binah was up before her father. Usually it took a little coaxing to rouse Binah from her nice warm bed. But today, her dad was lured to the kitchen by the smell of crispy bacon and fluffy scrambled eggs.

"Binah, what are you doing up so early?" her father exclaimed.

"I don't know. I couldn't really sleep." She ushered her father to a seat at the table and placed a heaping plate in front of him. "Coffee, Papa?"

Mr. Rossi breathed in the delicious aroma. "Why yes—thank you!" He took a bite. "Mmm! Binah, where on earth did you learn to cook like this?" Binah smiled. Her father asked her the same thing after every delicious meal she prepared.

She poured hot coffee into her father's favorite mug. "I honestly don't know," she said, just like she always did.

"Well, you have a natural ability." Her father smiled. "You must have inherited it from your mother. We both know you certainly didn't get it from me!"

Binah laughed with her dad, whose idea of a gourmet meal usually involved two things: macaroni and cheese.

"I'd like to think so. Did Mama cook for you a lot?"

"All the time," her father replied, smiling at the memory. "She knew she'd best not leave it up to me or we'd starve. Mmm . . . she made the most amazing beef stews. And freshly baked bread. The whole house would smell incredible. She was a joy to come home to."

Binah hovered over the stove. She loved hearing stories about her mother, who had passed away when Binah was very young. So young, she could barely even remember her. She wished she had more memories so she wouldn't have to play the same few over and over in her head. And even those seemed to be fading over time. But she didn't like to press her father for stories. He'd never said so, but she worried that talking about her mother made him sad. And making her father sad was the last thing on earth she ever wanted to do.

"Well, I'm glad you like it," she said, gently placing the coffee mug on the table and kissing her father on the cheek. "OK, Papa, I'm off."

"Already?" He looked at the clock. "But you still have time. Sit down, have a little breakfast."

Binah felt so jumpy, the thought of sitting down seemed actually impossible! "I want to get an early start today. You enjoy." She grabbed her school things. "I love you, Papa!"

"I love you too, Binah. Have a good day!"

"Well, someone has a lot of energy this morning! What's the occasion?" Grace asked when the rest of the English Roses came upon Binah waiting for them on the corner outside her house.

"Oh, I don't know," said Binah. A vision of Ben flitted through her mind. "I just . . ."

"You don't think we'll have a pop quiz to make up for not having one yesterday," Nicole interjected. "I really hope not. I mean, I studied, but not the way I would have if I'd known for sure we were having one."

"If we do, you know you'll ace it. Don't even," Charlotte replied.

Binah piped up again. "So, you guys. I have something to . . . well . . . yesterday at lunch . . ."

"GUYS!" Amy shrieked, pointing to an advertisement on a passing taxicab. "Look! Lizzie Love

is playing live in concert next week!" Lizzie Love was Amy's absolute favorite pop star. If you'd ever seen the posters covering the walls of her room, you'd know she was one hard-core fan! "We have to get tickets! We simply must go!"

The next few blocks passed in a flurry. Excitement about Lizzie Love led Amy to regale them with the latest celebrity gossip, which inspired Charlotte to fill them in on some star-inspired style tips. Nicole attempted to quiz them with her flash cards, while Grace juggled a football and tried to change the subject from school-talk. In no time, Hampstead School was before them.

With five best friends, there's always lots to talk about. Sometimes all the energy can make it difficult to see something—or someone—who's holding still. But just because one isn't making a lot of noise doesn't always mean one has nothing to say. Unfortunately, the English Roses could use a little practice in trying to hear what isn't being said out loud.

"Oh, Binah, you were saying something before," Grace remembered on their way through the doors. "Did you need to tell us something?"

The bell rang.

"No, that's OK," said Binah. "It was nothing."

CHAPTER 6

The Importance of Sketching Ernest

In first period, Binah raised her hand three times but was never called on. Once Mrs. Moss even looked around the room and said, "You mean to tell me no one knows the answer to number three? I'm disappointed, class." Binah looked up at her raised hand and wondered if she might actually be invisible.

In Lit class, Carole James had brought in cupcakes to celebrate her birthday. The class descended on the tray like a pack of hungry animals. Binah waited patiently until the crowd dispersed and was delighted to find a vanilla cupcake with pink icing still up for grabs. *This is a first!* thought Binah happily as she reached for the treat. Her reluctance to fight the crowd usually left her with the least desirable flavors.

"Oh, would you mind trading cupcakes, Binah?" asked Marvin Maples. "I'm allergic to chocolate."

Binah looked down at her pink cupcake. She really wanted that pink cupcake.

"Of course not," she said, and handed it to him. "It's all yours."

By the time lunch rolled around, Binah was feeling very tired. It didn't help that a soft drizzle had begun misting the windows and the sky was dark. She didn't feel much like eating.

"You guys go ahead," she told her friends as they gathered their things to head to the cafeteria. "I'll just be a minute."

The students filed out, and Binah was left alone. Even Mrs. Moss rushed out to the teachers' lounge, turning off the light behind her. Binah sighed. Somehow she wasn't surprised.

She turned the light back on and stood alone in the center of the room. *If I left and never ever came back, no one would even notice,* she thought. She walked over to Ernest's cage. He scurried round and round in his wire wheel, running infinitely to nowhere. *Hey, little guy,* she thought. *Mind some company?* She sat down and pulled a sketch notebook from her bag.

With each mark of the charcoal pencil against the creamy white page, Binah's spirits raised. Ernest's little eyes appeared on the sheet before her, then his tiny twitching nose, then his whiskers and furry ears. She sketched his tail and padded paws, and smiled as he reached up to take a drink from the water spout in the corner of his cage. She drew the contours of his fur with confident strokes.

"Wow. That's really good."

Binah started. Her hand flew to cover the page.

"You're not going to throw a condiment at me, are you? I come in peace!"

She blushed. Ben leaned over and gently moved her hand away.

"That's amazing. It's so real looking."

Binah blushed harder.

"I didn't hear you . . . I was just . . . fooling around. I'm really not . . ."

"You are," Ben insisted, looking back and forth from her drawing to Ernest in his cage. "I almost don't know which is which! Stop me if I accidentally feed the wrong one."

Binah couldn't help herself—she giggled. Ben smiled.

"Do you take lessons?" he asked, gesturing to her drawing.

"No." Binah shook her head. "It's just something I've always liked to do. My father says . . ." Her voice trailed off.

"What?" Ben asked.

"Nothing. Just, my mother liked to paint. So."

"Must be in your genes," Ben offered.

"Maybe," Binah returned.

"May I?" Ben reached for her notepad. Binah felt panicked. She'd never let anyone see her sketches. Of course she'd done pictures for her friends, and her father, and they claimed to love them, but . . . they had to say that! And before she could stop

ernest
by Binah
Rossi
Sketches
By
Binah

him, Ben was slowly flipping through the pages.

"Binah, these are great. You must really like animals."

It was true. She did. The notebook was filled with drawings of Nicole's dog, Amy's fish . . . even Charlotte's pet pony!

"Yes," said Binah quietly.

"Me too! I have two dogs, a chinchilla, a lizard, a kinkajou, and three Alaskan mice; and my sister has a parakeet. What pets do you have?"

Binah faltered. "I—well, actually, I don't have any."

"Really? That's too bad. I bet you'd take really good care of them. I can tell about those things."

Binah felt a really good feeling wash over her. She'd never felt anything quite like it before.

"You should come over and meet my animals. Sometime. If you want to," Ben continued hesitantly.

If the end-of-lunch bell hadn't rung right at that moment, Binah thought her heart might actually beat right out of her chest! She could almost picture it flopping around like a fish out of water on the floor in front of her. She suppressed a giggle at the thought.

"I'd like that," she said. "Very much."

Binah loves to wander the museum.

CHAPTER 7

A Halo of Frizz

Sometimes, something exciting happens to someone. And somehow, the fact that it's sort of a secret makes it extra-special. And then it almost seems like if it stops being a secret, it won't be quite as exceptional anymore.

Which could explain why Binah went through the rest of the day with a small smile on her face, and why she was still smiling as she waited under

the front awning of Hampstead School for her friends to meet her for the rainy ride home. She was actually rather glad that she hadn't gotten the chance to tell the Roses about Ben. This way, she could revel in her special little secret.

Alone with her thoughts, she pulled out her sketchbook. And smiling to herself, she let the knowledge of her sort-of secret guide her hand as she sketched a little something for a certain someone. She wasn't even really thinking about it. She just felt happy, and when Binah was happy, she drew.

She glanced up as she noticed some familiar shoes jog past her down the front stairs. *Just do it,* she said to herself. *Say hi!* She took a deep breath. "Hey, Ben—"

Just as Ben started to turn, Binah was jostled out of the way and a gust of sweet-smelling perfume wafted by. There was Evelyn Eaves, wearing an extremely short, extremely bright yellow dress. Her high heels had ribbons that tied around her ankles, and they clicked on the concrete as she scurried past. "Sorry, sweetie!" she called over her

shoulder. She flashed a quick wave; her nails were painted a dark, dark red—almost black. A high ponytail of shiny brown hair bounced behind her. A group of wide-eyed boys scuttled after her.

"Evelyn, do you want to borrow my class notes?" called one.

"Let me walk you home!" cried another.

"Evelyn, can I carry your books?!?" pleaded a third.

"I thought I told you to walk ten paces behind me," Evelyn singsonged over her shoulder. "If I can hear you, you're too close!"

The boys obediently stopped in their tracks, then followed eagerly behind her at a distance.

Binah watched the spectacle in awe. And then she froze.

Ben stood in the rain, his face turned as he looked for whoever had just called his name. His glasses slid down his nose, and he ran a hand through his shaggy hair.

Binah watched, helpless, as Evelyn Eaves leaned over Ben's shoulder. Her dark eyelashes batted next to him, and he looked up. She could not hear what they were saying. She could only see Evelyn Eaves's hand on Ben's arm. See Evelyn Eaves throw back her head in a confident giggle. See Evelyn Eaves lean in and kiss Ben on the cheek!

Binah could take no more. Her heart clenched, as did her fist.

How could I have been so stupid?! She crumpled the paper in her hand and as there was no wastebasket nearby, hurled it to the ground. *How could I ever think he liked me? I'm such an idiot!*

She ran inside and shot through the hallway at lightning speed, pushing past Nicole, who had just come to meet her. Not even sure where she was going, she darted around the corner with her blonde hair flying behind her as she tried to outrun her own tears. Maybe this sounds a wee bit dramatic, but wouldn't you react the same way if your Big Crush was suddenly kissed by another girl?

"Ooh, Binah! Helloo!"

Binah screeched to a halt at Miss Fluffernutter's feet. The teacher's face beamed with its usual flush, and her braided hair was a fluffy halo of frizz.

"Did you know? It's supposed to rain all next week. I know most people don't like the rain, but I actually find it can be rather delightful! Although it does wreak havoc with my hair." Even through her misery, Binah had to stifle a smile at that.

"Anyhoo, listen to me, babbling on. Babble babble babble! I do have a tendency to do that, don't I? Do you think anyone finds it charming? I hope so! I—"

And suddenly, she stopped short. For Miss

Fluffernutter noticed that something was not quite right with Binah.

"Binah, dear, are you all right?"

"Why? Don't I look all right? Don't I look nice?" Binah asked a bit sharply—which was highly out of character for her, as you might imagine.

"You just don't quite seem . . . yourself."

Binah frowned. "Maybe I don't want to be myself anymore."

"But why ever not? Yourself is a wonderful person to be!"

"Yeah, right."

Miss Fluffernutter put a comforting arm around her. "Is there something bothering you? You know, you can always come and talk to me. I'm here to listen."

Binah peered at her teacher through teary eyes and felt her heart drop a bit in her chest. She wanted to talk. She wanted to confess how stupid she'd been, how humiliated, how she could never show her face in public again.

Then she had a thought. Maybe she didn't have to! Not her old face, anyway.

"Thank you, Miss Fluffernutter!" Her voice had perked up considerably. "I appreciate that. But I'm fine, really."

As if to demonstrate that fact, she took her teacher's hand and spun out of her friendly embrace with a little twirl. "Nothing to worry about here!"

Miss Fluffernutter eyed her. "OK," she said. "I suppose I'll see you Monday, then!"

"Yes," said Binah, her eyes sparkling. "You will!"

And with that, she turned on her heel and sprinted from the scene, leaving poor Miss Fluffernutter even more befuddled than usual. And I don't think I have to tell you, that is pretty befuddled indeed.

CHAPTER 8

A Girl Thing

Since it was raining and he had the day off from work, Binah's father decided to pick his daughter up from school.

Just as he was walking up the front steps of Hampstead School, he was met by a fluster of friendly frizz coming down the stairs at the same time.

"Good afternoon, Mr. Rossi!"

"Yes, of course, Miss . . ." He was so distracted by the bundle of energy in front of him that he almost couldn't remember his daughter's favorite teacher's name. "Miss Fluffernutter!" He silently thanked his lucky stars he'd recollected that information before an embarrassing incident.

"Are you here about Binah?" she asked, attempting to stuff her hair into a rain bonnet. Which was no easy task, as the weather had caused her 'do to spring to about three times its former size.

"I thought I'd pick her up. Is she inside?" He started up the stairs, but a look on Miss Fluffernutter's face gave him pause. "Is something wrong?"

"Not wrong. No, no. Only . . . well, she just seemed a bit out of sorts when she left today."

"She did? How so? Is she sick?"

"Oh no," Miss Fluffernutter was quick to reassure him. "Nothing like that. I think it might be a . . . 'girl thing.' "

Mr. Rossi sighed. A girl thing? He feared he was not equipped for such problems, whatever they might be! "Is there anything I can do?" he implored Miss Fluffernutter. "At times like this I feel how much she needs a mother," he said wistfully. Miss Fluffernutter smiled in understanding, and the warmth in her kind eyes made him feel a wee bit better in spite of himself. He suddenly understood why she was Binah's favorite teacher.

"I'm sure you're doing a tip-top job," Miss Fluffernutter said. "There are just some things a girl needs to work out for herself. And with your support, I'm sure she will."

Mr. Rossi nodded. He was worried, but this fluffy, frizzy woman was quite convincing. As he headed home to meet his daughter, his nerves were eased by the knowledge that Miss Fluffernutter was looking out for them. And suddenly, he found he didn't much mind the rainy day.

It Rains
A Lot in LONDON
(But You
already Knew
That).

CHAPTER 9

The New Binah

"Get in, get in! I'm getting all wet!" Charlotte cried as Grace struggled to get into the sleek black car and close her umbrella at the same time.

On rainy days, Charlotte's driver—yes, Charlotte had a driver!—Royston drove the English Roses to school. If you've ever had to wait at the bus stop or walk in the pouring rain, you can appreciate just how nice that must be!

"Happy Monday," said Grace as they sped through the gloom.

"I'm almost glad the weekend's over!" Charlotte exclaimed. "It was just so dreary. School is practically a welcome relief!"

Royston whisked them off to Amy's house, then to Nicole's. By the time they got to Binah's, the inside of the car was so humid it felt like a greenhouse. The windows fogged up against the cold rain pattering against them, so the girls couldn't see anything outside.

But even if it had been clear as day, they never would have believed that the girl who opened the car door was their nice little Binah.

"Morning, girls!"

The greeting was met with shocked silence.

"What? Cat got your tongues?"

Binah's toes were polished a sparkly blue. Her legs were bare to the thigh, where the jagged edge of what looked like a hastily scissored-off dress hem began. The loud green fabric fluttered in the cold breeze that gusted into the car as she pulled the door closed behind her. Her brightly lipsticked lips curved into a smile. "Helloo? Anybody home?"

And then Amy said what they were all thinking. "Binah! Your . . . your hair!"

Binah's lovely, long blonde hair was now a shocking shade of black.

"You like? I did it myself."

"We can see that," Charlotte murmured.

Binah shot her a look.

"But . . . but why?" Amy asked, unable to contain herself. "Your hair was so pretty!"

"Yeah—pretty boring," Binah retorted.

"Aren't you freezing?" asked the ever-practical Nicole. Binah shook her head, but the goose bumps on her bare arms betrayed her.

"How on earth can you walk in those?" Grace pointed to the platform sandals that had to have had at least a three-inch heel.

"They're fine." Binah rolled her eyes.

"It's just—this doesn't seem like you," Charlotte pointed out the obvious. "Not at all."

"All right, enough with the third degree." Binah folded her arms. "This is me. The new me. Take it or leave it."

Walking into Hampstead School that morning,

introducing
THE
new
BINAH
!!!

Charlotte felt what it must be like to be in a celebrity entourage. She couldn't even count the number of people who stared at them as they passed, and burst into hushed whispers as they watched them walking by.

Nicole kept her head down. Truth be told, she was rather embarrassed. She ducked past the shocked stares and edged her friends toward the classroom as urgently as she could.

Amy was in a daze. What was Binah wearing? How could she possibly think this ensemble was a good idea? The dress was way too short and totally out of season. It was the ultimate "faux pas"—a phrase Amy had learned from her fashion-forward mother. It meant, in a nutshell, "huge, embarrassing mistake."

Grace didn't quite know what to think. She looked at Binah searchingly. Something must be really wrong to incite her to do something like this. Grace was not the girliest girl around, but even she knew a girl doesn't do something like that to her hair unless there's a very big reason.

Binah walked with her head held high. Her ankles wobbled a bit in her shoes, but she steadied herself without incident. Her hands subconsciously floated down to the hem of her dress, but she stopped herself from pulling it lower over her thighs. *This is the new Binah!* she thought. *Get used to it, world!* And even though she herself was about as far from "comfortable" as you can get, Binah finished the long walk to class with her nose in the air, her new black hair gleaming, and a crowd of speechless students in her wake. She most certainly was not "the nice one" today!

CHAPTER 10

In Her Shoes

To Mrs. Moss's credit, she managed to uphold an air of indifference when the English Roses walked into her homeroom. Binah expected a reaction. She was even prepared to get in trouble. But Mrs. Moss merely gave her one up-and-down look from behind her glasses and moved on, not glancing in her direction again.

By the time lunch rolled around, Binah was positively starving. She'd slipped out of the house before breakfast so her father wouldn't see her. Mrs. Moss may have held her tongue, but Binah had a suspicion that her father wouldn't have done the same thing.

She took an extra long time packing up when class ended.

"You guys go ahead," she said to her friends. "I'll meet you there." Ordinarily, they would have protested. But today Amy, Charlotte, Grace, and Nicole simply nodded and ran for the cafeteria.

Amy saw the teacher first. "Miss Fluffernutter!" she cried, and ran down the hall with her friends.

"Hello, girls! How are you?"

"We need your help!" Amy cried.

"Something's wrong with Binah!" said Nicole.

"She's acting really weird," Grace elaborated.

"And she's done something horrid to her hair!" Charlotte exclaimed.

Miss Fluffernutter pulled them into her empty classroom. "Calm down, girls. Where is Binah now?"

"She's still in class." Amy caught her breath. Just being in Miss Fluffernutter's room had her feeling better already. "She said she'd meet us at lunch. You have to help her. We don't know what to do!"

"She said it's the 'new her,' and we should get used to it," Charlotte continued. "But I don't think we can."

"Can you think of a reason Binah might want to change?"

"No! None at all!" chorused the girls.

"Binah's the best," said Grace.

"Yes, but do you ever tell her so?" asked Miss Fluffernutter.

The new-and-improved (and nice-as-ever) Binah

"All the time," Charlotte replied. "We're always saying 'That's Binah: the nice one.'"

"Hmm," Miss Fluffernutter murmured thoughtfully. "Binah is quite nice, isn't she?"

"Yes," confirmed Nicole. "She's always doing nice things for everyone and never says a word about it."

"Interesting . . ." Miss Fluffernutter rubbed her chin. "Do you think that maybe Binah's been feeling a little . . . taken for granted?"

The girls looked back at her, puzzled.

"What do you mean?" asked Nicole.

"Sometimes when someone is exceptionally nice, it's easy for their friends to rely on them to be that way all the time, no matter what. And they're so nice, they'd never want to remind their friends to say thank you. And to let them know how much they're appreciated."

The girls were quiet. Finally, Amy piped up, "I think maybe, that could possibly have been the case."

"But why would she go and do something like this?" asked Charlotte. "I mean, this is extreme."

"It does seem so, doesn't it? But Charlotte, when you're having a problem, whom do you ask for advice?"

"Besides my friends? Mum, of course," Charlotte said without hesitation. "She always knows what to say to make me feel better."

"And Amy, where do you get your fashion sense? Who taught you all your style tricks?"

"My mum," she replied. Next to the English Roses, her mother was her best friend.

"Grace, in a house full of brothers, your mum is a welcome woman's perspective. Am I right?"

Grace nodded. She loved her brothers, but she was glad she and her mom could have "girl time" when she needed a break from the boys!

"And Nicole, I know your mum stays up late studying with you whenever you need her. True?"

"She does. And she makes the best flash cards," Nicole added.

"It is a wonderful thing to have great friends in one's life. But there is no substitute for a mother, is there?"

The English Roses shook their heads.

"As Binah's best friends, you'll know better than anyone when she might need a mother most. And then you can be there for her even more than usual, to help her through it since her mum can't."

The girls looked at one another, finally understanding. Miss Fluffernutter was always excep-

tionally good at putting things in perspective and helping them to see that sometimes, in order to understand someone, you need to put yourself in their shoes. That way, you can start to see what they're going through, even if you yourself have never experienced anything like it.

"Binah is very lucky to have friends like you. As you're so lucky to have her. And I'm lucky to know all of you! Now you know you can always come talk to me about anything, no matter what."

"We know," Grace said. "Thank you—this is a terrific help."

The girls exchanged a look.

"And now, if you'll excuse us," Amy said, "I think we have some 'being-there' to do!"

CHAPTER II

Not So Boring

Dinah was on the lookout. She sat in Mrs. Moss's empty classroom, fidgeting with her books and her bags, peeking at the little window over the door to see if she could spot some dark brown hair through the glass. She was about to give up hope when suddenly, there he was!

"Hi," said Ben. "Oh, I'm sorry, never mind. I was looking for . . ."

Binah turned toward him. Ben blanched.

"Binah? Is that you?"

OK, this is it, Binah thought. *This is the New You!*

No more "nice one." That's not how the game is played.

"Um, who else would it be?" she asked in what she thought was a coy, flirty voice. It sounded a little harsh to her ears, but she just chalked that up to the fact that she wasn't used to it. Yet.

"Oh. Wow. You look . . ."

"Yeah?" Binah prompted.

"Different."

"Hmm. OK then."

Silence followed.

"Soooo." Binah twirled a lock of newly black hair around her finger.

"I was just going to feed Ernest. Do you . . . want to help?"

"Help? Feed a gerbil? Ew! No thanks. Hee hee!" She tried to giggle girlishly, but it sounded stiff and fake and caught in her throat. She was going to have to practice this "be mean to boys so they'll like you" thing. It obviously didn't come naturally!

"Oh. OK."

Silence again. Binah wasn't exactly sure what she

was supposed to do next. But in her plan, she figured Ben should be begging her to be his girlfriend right about now. She waited.

"Well, I'll see you later then."

This wasn't exactly the response she'd been hoping for.

"Oh. You don't want to . . . ask me anything?" She batted her eyelashes, and mascara flaked off into her eye. Ouch.

"What . . . what should I be asking?" Ben looked genuinely confused.

Binah walked toward him, her eye burning. "Oh, I don't know. You're supposed to be so smart, can't you figure it out?"

Ben went from looking confused to looking rather afraid!

"Sorry . . . I'm not really sure what you're talking about. And I, uh, I gotta go."

And before she could stop him with her ravishing new looks or flirty mean-girl banter, Ben was gone. She stared after him, mouth open, wondering what went wrong. This had not gone according to plan. Not one bit!

"Binah!" Grace, Nicole, Amy, and Charlotte burst into the room.

"We know what's going on!"

"Don't you know we think you're the best?"

"You're perfect just the way you are!"

"We'd be lost without you!"

Binah, bowled over by their energy, fell into a chair.

"We're sorry if we've taken you for granted!"

"We so appreciate everything you do for us!"

Binah didn't know what to say. Suddenly, all the confidence of New Binah sputtered out of her like a deflating balloon, leaving her wilted and exhausted. She put her head down on the desk.

"Binah. Please tell us what's wrong." Nicole reached out and put a hand on her arm. Binah's shoulders raised and lowered in a huge, pained sigh.

"I was just . . ." She took a deep breath. "I was

tired of just being 'the nice one.'" Grace, you're a tremendous athlete. Nicole, you're so smart and driven. Amy, you have such confidence and style. Charlotte, everyone's drawn to your dramatic personality. And I'm . . . nothing! Boring, bland . . . and nice."

She sniffled. The other girls looked down.

"But then . . . there was this boy. Ben." Binah gulped. Saying his name out loud took all the wind out of her. She looked down at her hands and continued. "He seemed like he maybe . . . liked me." She rolled her eyes, which were brimming with tears. "So stupid! Of course he didn't. He was just being nice to 'nice old Binah.' So I thought I'd throw the old me away. Become someone new. Someone better. Someone exciting. Someone . . ."

"... not so nice," finished Amy.

"Yeah. And now . . . and now I've gone and ruined everything!"

Amy nodded. "I understand." Binah looked up at her.

"You do?"

"Of course we do!" echoed Charlotte. The other girls nodded in agreement.

"You know what? I think I have the answer to this problem." Amy grinned. "Girls, gather round. I have a plan."

CHAPTER 12

Roses to the Rescue!

Binah stared in the mirror, her friends bustling around her within the confine of the girls' bathroom. "Well, you may have gone a bit overboard, Binah, but you have great instincts! This is definitely your color," Amy said, fiddling with her dress. "It really suits you. I'm just lowering the hem to . . . here!" She pinned

a swath of matching fabric (her key to the costume room had come in mighty handy!) right above the knee. Binah thought this was a very sensible—yet very flattering—length.

Charlotte set to work pinning her hair back. "There. Now it looks . . . less severe," she said, working her magic.

"It's not permanent," Binah said.

"That's probably good. Your natural color is really gorgeous. I've always been jealous of it," Charlotte admitted.

"You have?"

"Yeah! Don't look so surprised," she said, smiling at the expression on Binah's face.

"Binah, you could dye your hair green and you'd still look great!" Grace declared loyally.

Charlotte leaned in. "I wouldn't go that far!" she whispered.

"Seriously, though," Grace continued. "New hair, new clothes, all of that's great. But here's the thing." She met Binah's eyes in the mirror. "Be yourself. But be the best of yourself. And don't be afraid to go after what you want, because you deserve it." She smiled. "And if anyone ever forgets that, you have my permission to remind them. Us included!"

"OK, Binah!" Nicole burst into the bathroom and took Binah by the hand. "Is she ready, girls?"

"Definitely," Charlotte, Amy, and Grace agreed. And off they went.

CHAPTER 13

One More Surprise

Binah looked at the clock, watching the second hand *tick, tick, tick* away. Why her friends had left her alone in their classroom with express instructions not to move, she could not understand.

Binah tapped her fingers on her desk and smoothed her hands over her new dress. Finally, she opened her bag to get out her sketch pad. Peering inside, she rifled around but couldn't seem to find it. So intent was she in her search that she didn't hear the door open or notice someone come in.

"Hey."

Binah looked up. Her eyes widened. "Oh! Hi."

Ben walked closer. "I'm looking for Binah. Do you know if she's here?"

Binah smiled shyly. "I think I might be able to find her for you."

"Yeah? That would be great. Because . . ." He paused.

"Because . . . why?" Binah asked tentatively.

"Well . . . she's really . . ."

"Nice?" Binah offered.

"Yes, she's definitely nice. But also funny. And interesting."

"Yeah. Not as interesting as Evelyn Eaves." Binah looked down.

Ben rolled his eyes. "Interesting? More like annoying. She's always trying to get me to do her homework. She found out I'm kind of good at math and now she thinks I'm her ticket to 'A-plus City!'"

"Oh!" said Binah. And this time "Oh" was enough!

"Anyway." Ben reached into his pocket and pulled out a crumpled piece of paper. Binah gasped—it was the drawing she'd intended to give

THE
NEW NEW
BINAH

to him before things had gone so terribly awry.

"If you see Binah, would you tell her I have this? Her friends found it and gave it to me. I'd give it back, but I'm hoping she'll let me keep it."

"Really? Why?" Binah asked.

"She's a great artist. It'll probably be worth something some day!"

Binah laughed. "I'll tell her. Anything else you want me to let her know?"

"Maybe just . . . that I miss seeing her around. It's been nice getting to know her."

Grace's advice echoed in Binah's head. *Be yourself and don't be afraid,* she repeated silently to herself. She took a deep breath.

"It's been nice getting to know you, too," Binah said confidently. And Ben blushed!

Binah burst into laughter. "Come on," she said. "Wanna grab some food before lunch is over?"

Ben nodded. "I'd like that."

"Just have to do one thing first," said Binah. She walked over to Ernest's cage and held out a food pellet. The hungry gerbil eagerly scampered over and nibbled it right out of her hand.

Ben smiled. "You're a natural!" he exclaimed. "I hereby appoint you Co-Official Class Gerbil Feeder! If you're up for the challenge . . ."

Binah grinned. "I accept with honor."

And with that, the two of them walked out into the hall.

Binah smiled to herself, overwhelmed with the events of her incredibly eventful day. But she was in for one more surprise!

Stepping out into the hallway, she saw her friends smiling at her eagerly. Then she met the eyes of her father! He was standing next to Miss Fluffernutter, and the two of them looked pleased as punch about something.

"Papa!" Binah exclaimed. "What are you doing here?"

"I have something for you. And I was told it couldn't wait another minute. In fact, according to your friends, I've been very remiss in not having given this to you sooner." The English Roses nodded emphatically. Then, out from behind his back, Binah's father pulled a medium-sized box with small holes poked all over the surface. "Well, go on," Mr. Rossi coaxed. "Open it!"

Binah tore away the wrapping and opened the

box. When she saw what was inside, she let out a yelp of glee. There it was: the cutest, furriest, most adorable little gerbil she had ever seen! "Papa! I love him!"

"It's a her, actually," said Miss Fluffernutter, stepping forward. Smiling, she and Mr. Rossi locked eyes. *Hmmm,* Binah thought. *Maybe I'm not the only one having a good day.*

Ben picked up the furry little animal and held her out for Binah to hold. "Your first pet! Now, you need to make an extremely important decision." He paused dramatically. "What are you gonna name her?"

Binah smiled and thought for a moment. "I don't know. I've never done this before! What do you think?"

Ben smiled at her and scrunched his glasses up on his nose. "How about . . . Ernesta?"

Binah grinned. "That sounds . . ." She paused and looked around. Charlotte blew her a kiss. Grace gave a thumbs-up. Nicole nodded encouragingly. Amy winked. Her father and Miss Fluffernutter glanced shyly at each other and then beamed at her.

Binah threw out her arms and laughed a beautiful, open, wonderfully confident laugh. "That sounds nice!"

And it was. It was very nice, indeed!

The End

Previous Books by Madonna

PICTURE BOOKS:

The English Roses
Mr. Peabody's Apples
Yakov and the Seven Thieves
The Adventures of Abdi
Lotsa de Casha
The English Roses: Too Good To Be True

CHAPTER BOOKS:

Friends For Life!
Good-Bye, Grace?
The New Girl
A Rose by Any Other Name
Big-Sister Blues

MADONNA RITCHIE was born in Bay City, Michigan, and now lives in London and Los Angeles with her husband, movie director Guy Ritchie, and her children, Lola, Rocco, and David. She has recorded 17 albums and appeared in 18 movies. This is the sixth in her series of chapter books. She has also written six picture books for children, starting with the international bestseller *The English Roses,* which was released in 40 languages and more than 100 countries.

JEFFREY FULVIMARI was born in Akron, Ohio. He started coloring when he was two, and has never stopped. Soon after graduating from The Cooper Union in New York City, he began drawing for magazines and television commercials around the globe. He currently lives in a log cabin in upstate New York, and is happiest when surrounded by stacks of paper and magic markers.

A NOTE ON THE TYPE:

This book is set in Mazarin, a "humanist" typeface designed by Jonathan Hoefler. Mazarin is a revival of the typeface of Nicolas Jenson, the fifteenth-century typefounder who created one of the first roman printing types.